MW00800333

HOBBLEDY-CLOP

by Pat Brisson

Illustrated by Maxie Chambliss

For Baby Smith ~
Welcome to the world!
Come join the party!
Pat Brisson
♡ 2008

Boyds Mills Press

For the RiverStone Writers:
Denise Brunkus, Sally M. Keehn, Joyce McDonald,
Trinka Hakes Noble, Pamela Curtis Swallow, and Elvira Woodruff,
with fond memories of our many tea parties.
—P. B.

To our little Grammy who loved a nice cup of tea and a visit.
—M. C.

Text copyright © 2003 by Pat Brisson
Illustrations copyright © 2003 by Maxie Chambliss
All rights reserved

Boyds Mills Press, Inc.
A Highlights Company
815 Church Street
Honesdale, Pennsylvania 18431

Visit our Web site at www.boydsmillspress.com

Printed in China

Publisher Cataloging-in-Publication Data
Brisson, Pat.
Hobbledy-clop / by Pat Brisson ; illustrated by
Maxie Chambliss.—1st ed.
[32] p. : col. ill. ; cm.
Summary: A young boy is joined by his animal friends as he and his
little red wagon go up the hill to Grandma's house.
ISBN 1-56397-888-1
1. Animals—Fiction. I. Chambliss, Maxie. II. Title
[E] 21   AC   2003
2002108411

First edition, 2003

Book design by Amy Drinker, Aster Designs
The text of this book is set in 16-point Bookman.
The illustrations are done in watercolor.

10 9 8 7 6 5 4 3 2 1

Brendan O'Doyle was on the way to his grandmother's house. He was bringing a tea party in his little red wagon. Hobbledy-clop, hobbledy-clop went the wagon over the bumps in the road. Hobbledy-clop, hobbledy-clop up the road to Grandma's.

Brendan's snake, Dudley, felt the ground rumble. He slithered from his rock in the sun and stared at Brendan in silence. Brendan knew exactly what that stare meant.

"I'm taking a tea party to Grandma's," explained Brendan. "You may join me if you'd like, but try not to tickle."

So Brendan O'Doyle (with Dudley wrapped carefully around his arm) and the little red wagon hobbledy-clopped and hobbledy-clopped up the road to Grandma's.

Brendan's dog, Atlas, smelled the cookies
and came running.

"Woof! Woof!" said Atlas.

Brendan knew exactly what that bark meant. "No," explained Brendan.

"The cookies are for the party. You may join us if you'd like, but *you'll* have to carry Dudley. And be careful, because he likes to tickle, especially elbows."

So Brendan O'Doyle, Atlas the dog (with
Dudley riding bareback), and the little red wagon
hobbledy-clopped and hobbledy-clopped up the
road to Grandma's.

Brendan's cat, Beatrice, smelled the milk and padded from the barn.

"Meow! Meow!" said Beatrice the cat.

Brendan knew exactly what that meow meant. "No," explained Brendan. "The milk is for the party. You may join us if you'd like, but *you'll* have to carry Dudley. And be careful, because he likes to tickle, especially ears."

So Brendan O'Doyle, Atlas the dog, Beatrice the cat (wearing Dudley like a necklace), and the little red wagon hobbledy-clopped and hobbledy-clopped up the road to Grandma's.

Brendan's pony, Corabelle, smelled the sugar
and trotted from the field.

"Neigh! Neigh!" said Corabelle.

Brendan knew exactly what that neigh meant.
"No," explained Brendan. "The sugar is for the party.
You may join us if you'd like, but *you'll* have to
carry Dudley. And be careful, because he likes to
tickle, especially chins."

So Brendan O'Doyle, Atlas the dog, Beatrice the cat, Corabelle the pony (with Dudley braided through her mane), and the little red wagon hobbledy-clopped and hobbledy-clopped up the road to Grandma's.

Grandma was weeding in her garden when
they arrived.

"My goodness!" said Grandma.
"What have we here?"

"Surprise!" said Brendan.

"It's a tea party!"

"A tea party!" said Grandma.

"What could be better?"

Brendan spread the tablecloth and poured tea for two. Atlas the dog gulped down his cookies in a twinkling and begged for pieces from everyone else. Beatrice the cat lapped milk from a saucer with her sandpapery tongue and purred contentedly.

Corabelle the pony nibbled sugar cubes and
nuzzled Brendan's pockets for more. Grandma, who
loved to be tickled, held Dudley the snake.

Dudley tickled
Grandma's elbows.
Grandma giggled.

Dudley tickled
Grandma's ears.
Grandma giggled.

Dudley tickled Grandma's cheeks and nose, and Grandma giggled and giggled. She giggled so hard, her hat fell off.

When Brendan O'Doyle saw his grandmother
giggling, he giggled, too. He giggled so hard, he knocked
over the empty teapot. When Grandma and
Brendan saw that, they giggled even harder,
and Brendan knocked over the milk. Grandma
giggled so hard, her glasses slipped down her nose.

Brendan giggled so hard, three
cookies slipped from his plate

and plopped onto Atlas's head.
Atlas barked in surprise.

Beatrice meowed along with him.

Corabelle whinnied and neighed.

Dudley, who had caused all the fuss, slithered off Grandma's lap and into the empty teapot, where he soon fell fast asleep.

When they finally stopped giggling, Brendan and Grandma sighed with pleasure and agreed it was the best tea party ever.

Soon it was time to go. Brendan and his grandmother packed up the little red wagon—

and kissed each other good-bye.

Then Brendan O'Doyle, Atlas the dog, Beatrice the cat, Corabelle the pony, and the little red wagon (with Dudley riding safely in the empty teapot) hobbledy-clopped and hobbledy-clopped all the way home.